ALLEN COUNTY PUBLIC LIBRARY

FORT WAYNE, INDIANA 46802

You may return this book to any agency, branch,
or bookmobile of the Allen County Public Library.

DEMCO

Views from Valley Front

by Beatrice Jefferson Stubbs

JOHN F. BLAIR, Publisher
Winston-Salem, North Carolina

Composition by Greensboro Printing Company
Manufactured by BookCrafters

Library of Congress Cataloging in Publication Data
Stubbs, Beatrice Jefferson.
Views from Valley Front.
I. Title.
PS3569.T829V5   1986   814'.54   86-12904
ISBN 0-89587-053-3 (pbk.)

To My

Grandchildren

God gave all men all earth to love,
    But, since our hearts are small,
Ordained for each one spot should prove
    Beloved over all.

Rudyard Kipling, "Sussex"

Table of Contents

Views from Valley Front

Views from Valley Front

T he superhighway had stretched into a long day's drive when, at last, over the crest of a hill I caught sight of the mountains. I was home. I was in my own bailiwick, even though I was still more than a hundred miles from the house my husband and I had built when my health made it imperative to leave the low country and move to the mountains, where I seemed to thrive and where I now live alone.

As the mountains loomed in an irregular gray line against a colorless sky, all the sentiments embodied in the word *home* caused me to press my foot on the accelerator, hoping I would not meet the highway patrol. My eye cast a line toward those rugged ridges and my heart raced over it with the speed of light. I took a deep breath of mountain air with its special ingredient that awakens energy and revives a reason for living.

I was returning after three happy months in Tidewater, Virginia, where gracious living is still practiced and where I have relatives and roots that go back to the early days of the colonies. So why this elation at returning to a solitary existence on the side of a mountain with responsibilities and a lot of plain hard work awaiting me?

A person is lucky when, at some point in his life, he stumbles on a spot that strikes a responsive chord, where he immediately feels comfortable, where he instinctively knows that here he can relate to the universal and discover his miniscule role in the midst of the welter and confusion of today's world. For some that place is the seashore, for others the sweep of the prairies, and I have a niece who draws inspiration from the arid deserts of the West. For me the mystique of the mountains not only improves my metabolism but speaks of the greatness of God, the Creative Energy expressing itself in trees beyond counting, in spectacular water- falls, in the fullness of distant vistas, and in the forests with their precious blossoms of early spring. I like being a part of it all.

Intent on the road, I paid little attention to the mountains as my car started to climb, but I was conscious of their presence, and I felt vitality re- turning and my heart beating with a joy for which there were no words.

It was late on a windy March day when I arrived at my red-and-white house, which friends describe as having "good vibrations," the result of the rip- ened love of our retirement years, which still lingers years after my husband's death. On that dour day, the view from the terrace, if one were seeing it for the first time, could only be described as drab. Nevertheless, to me it was soul-satisfying. I ignored the fact that my familiar mountains were in one of their moods. They were there, and I loved them.

When I send snapshots to distant friends, they comment that my scenes might have been taken in New Hampshire or Vermont. An accurate appraisal. The Appalachians begin to peter out as they reach Georgia, and space for pleasant valleys, such as one finds in New England, is left in between. While these mountains are not so tall as many directly to

4

the north, they are big enough—true mountains with altitudes between two thousand and three thousand feet. Their positions may be fixed, but their appearance changes from moment to moment depending on clouds and sunlight. Their reassuring permanence is one of their attractions, but I have watched them when they seemed to be in motion, racing with buffalo clouds driven by the wind. In summer I have caught them stretched out sleeping in a hypnotic haze. Their unpredictable colors range from milky white at dawn to a medley of greens at noon and the deep blue of lapis lazuli after the sun goes down.

My house faces west, looking across a fertile valley toward larger mountains. Its location gives me a ringside seat for dramatic sunsets—always exciting, always different. And while I glory in these intense displays, there is another time of day I prefer.

On a clear morning in winter at about 7:00, as the planet is turning on its axis, it receives the first rays of the sun that rises back of my house and sends light to brush the tips of the tall mountains across the valley with a soft, delicate pink—the color of a wild rose. This lasts but a few moments for as the sun continues its climb, the pink gives way to clear white light, and by 7:05 the show is over. The unexpectedness is what makes it memorable. Pink is considered a feminine color, and it is not usual to ascribe feminine attributes to mountains. That rosy glow, so brief, carries over into the rest of the day.

At the foot of my sloping lawn is a field—fifteen acres more or less—which makes good scenery in every season, but especially in early spring when tractors expose red Georgia clay on a slope near the road and rich brown soil in the bottoms. Beyond is the Little Tennessee River, which rises over in Wolk

Fork Valley and by the time it reaches here is already a small river. The field is rented by an absentee owner and planted year after year in corn, to the delight of the canny crows, who wait till the planters have departed and then go systematically down row after row enjoying every kernel not well covered.

In July when the corn is in tassel, it is heaven for honeybees. In this area sourwood honey is the choice of tourists. Sourwood trees bloom when the corn is in tassel, and our county agent, a bee-man himself, wryly speculates that much of the honey labeled sourwood may contain corn nectar since both are clear and golden and impossible to distinguish. Sourwood has the dominant flavor, so the corn nectar may be absorbed as filler. Only the bees know for sure, and they don't communicate. However, the purchaser is not really defrauded with the mixture because it is delicious.

The river cuts clean across the field and is spanned by a wooden bridge, sagging and dubious, which one crosses on faith or triples the mileage into the village. Another field on the far side is rented for cabbages. Machines come in to plant this well-paying crop and make even-distanced rows which provide a different shade of grayish green to our palette of colors.

Beyond that field runs a small stream in which beavers claim a vested interest and keep up perpetual warfare with the county crew by damming the drain under the road. I have seen as many as ten workmen leaning on their shovels cogitating how to outwit those beavers, who go right back to work at closing the drain as soon as the men depart. At this point the welcome pavement begins that runs four-tenths of a mile to the main highway.

All these fields lie directly in front of my house, and when the land beyond the river was sold, it was rumored that a promoter would use it for a bluegrass park. This sounded good to me, for being from Kentucky originally, I regarded the term *bluegrass* as both revered and nostalgic. However, I soon learned that in the modern vernacular it described rock or country music and all that this implies. My heart sank, but I gave myself a stern lecture about accepting change and was rewarded by the news that the land was found to be too low, too often flooded, for that use, and the project was abandoned. A golf driving range was a welcome substitute.

I can count a half dozen sizable mountains directly on the far side of the highway and an incalculable number of more massive ones marching toward the western horizon. A stunning view in any season. When I look intently, the mountains give the impression of encircling arms. They make me feel safe.

A view is the first thing a person demands in buying mountain property. Realtors recognize this and capitalize on it; necessities such as water, roads, and sewerage are secondary. The view's the thing, and rightly so because a panorama of thousands of acres upon which one pays no taxes is unearned wealth indeed! A buyer may not be able to explain why he wants a mountain place, but something tells him he must have a view. Once settled, he finds that his view is the stage setting from which the mountains speak and from which he draws the benefits they have to bestow.

The importance of views is even recognized by the Highway Department, which has made turnouts where motorists may park and punctuate their trip with sweeping vistas. At such places one hears little beyond "wonderful," "magnificent," "breathtaking," "beautiful," but when these adjectives have been exhausted, the impact felt, the cars are likely to pull out with silent passengers.

People are coming to our mountains in increasing numbers. Tourism accounts for the many shops and eating places mushrooming along the highways. Small towns are growing apace, and clerks in courthouses are busy recording deeds. What draws these visitors, and why are so many staying?

A superficial answer could be climate, change, or recreation, but I feel there is a more subtle reason. In this generation man's universe has been expanded in time and space to mind-boggling proportions, and within it the tempo of life has accelerated out of control. No matter how disciplined man tries to be, he is subjected to pressures from all sides. He needs to escape, if only for a short time. The more complex life becomes the greater the quest for its meaning. The enduring mountains, with their reservoir of time, offer answers. They soar above the complexities of daily life, and in their company man's fretful anxieties are cut down to size, while at the same time his own worth is affirmed.

As a longtime resident I have formulated my own theory to explain the lure of the mountains, but I wanted to validate it before putting it into print. I got my clue from a friend from Macon, Georgia, who said that he stopped to fill his gas tank in the valley, but on the climb to Highlands, when he came to the Blue Valley Overlook, he stopped to fill his soul. That was it. Mountains nourish our spirits.

I had also come to the conclusion that people look at mountains not so much with their eyes as with their hearts, that they feel more intensely than they visualize. So I casually began tossing out this simple question: "What comes into your mind the instant you catch the first glimpse of the mountains?"

Here is a fair sampling of the answers:

A middle-aged man, whose face registered grim acceptance of life's frustrations, eased into a smile as he replied, "I love 'em. They make me feel good. I wish I could live here."

His wife, a secretary in a South Georgia courthouse, spoke up: "I say 'Praise the Lord' out loud. Mountains make it easy to believe in God."

A New York career girl, working in the theater, did not take long to think. "It's the vastness that gets to me. The mountains replenish my spirit. If it weren't for this annual visit, I doubt if I could continue day after day facing tall walls."

A friend, recently widowed, looked into the distance and said, "When I return, the mountains seem like a benediction—like 'the peace that passeth all understanding.' But," she added, "they also accentuate my loneliness. We had such joy sharing them."

A single, middle-aged professor laughingly admitted he sometimes speaks out loud. "You're still there, Old Things, even though I haven't been thinking of you." And then he added, "It's like coming home from college for vacation when you're all hot and bothered over whether you passed that exam or whether your girl is dating someone else. Then you see your father and mother standing on the porch to welcome you. All your anxieties vanish. You're home safe."

An Atlanta salesman said, "I know it won't be long before I'm in my cabin in the woods in utter quiet—no city noises—only the music of the rain on my tin roof. It's worth the long drive up."

More than any other response was the word *peace*.
A few said *tranquillity*. Everyone to whom I put the
question voiced an emotional reaction rather than a
physical description; probably none could have
drawn a picture of what they were seeing. There
was one exception—as there always must be to any
blanket generalization. A young New York artist,
when asked the same question, replied, "I see
shapes, colors, and relationships." *He* was using his
eyes and expressing his craft, but I noted that his
canvas carried pent-up city emotions. The scene he
was painting, which seemed to me to be a gentle
June pastel with the delicacy of a watercolor, he
depicted in tropical colors with Gauguinesque sever-
ity.

These responses spoke for themselves. The lens
of the eye took instant impressions and rushed the
film to be developed in the heart with the speed of a
Polaroid camera. These people had been drawn to
the mountains for a multitude of reasons, each
reflecting individual needs. I was surprised none
had mentioned what I consider an important factor,
namely, the absence of man in sweeping mountain
views. For it is the human element, the strain and
stress of constant contact with people in business
and at home, that causes trouble. Here there seems
to be elbowroom to be alone, a reprieve from pres-
sure, and a sense of time—not man-calculated time
but endless time suggested by the mountains themselves. All this is good medicine.

What I read into these varied responses is that
mountains evoke man's unconscious seeking for
"something beyond," that as the eye travels vertically
towards the peaks, it draws the mind away from
daily cares and towards the infinite. From time
immemorial mountains have been a symbol of the

10

dwelling place of God. There have been holy mountains and magic mountains in all recorded history.

However it is worded, it becomes apparent that mountains continue to "speak" to man. Let no one assume, however, that living in the mountains makes an Eden. Here there are just as many power failures, plumbing crises, dead batteries, frustrating workmen, family disputes, long rainy seasons or nervous droughts, *plus* chiggers and poison ivy.

But all the while there is the backdrop of the mountains to calm the spirit, to give proportion to petty problems as we "lift up our eyes unto the hills."

Summer Wild Flowers

What Abraham Lincoln said about common people is equally true of summer wild flowers. He said the Lord must have loved them because he made so many of them. The chief characteristic of the wild flowers that grace our roadsides, fill our fence rows, and invade our gardens from June until the first fall frost is their prodigal fertility—their massive numbers. One single dandelion begets hundreds of little dandelions, as owners of well-groomed lawns know only too well. All the wild flowers that add to our summer scenery multiply like mad. Too much of a good thing results in their being downgraded and called weeds.

Some of my favorite flowers are these so-called weeds. I can think of nothing cooler looking on a hot July day than a clear vase of Queen Anne's lace and ferns. Volunteer daisies and black-eyed Susans in the flower beds supply cut flowers for the house. I depend on them.

From my back porch I can look at a bank devoted solely to summer wild flowers. This was an afterthought, or rather the result of watching the habits and demands of the flowers themselves. I had observed that the first heralds of spring—violets, hepaticas, bloodroot, trilliums, and their ilk—all bloom before the trees put forth their leaves so that they may benefit from the weak April sun and come to blossom, develop seeds, and ensure the continuation of the species. Accordingly, I planted these early bloomers in a wooded area in deep leaf mold, where they could lie dormant in shade during the summer heat.

I had likewise noted that by the time the trees come to full leaf, the familiar summer flowers have chosen to avoid shade and settled in full sun. Moreover, they seemed not to require good soil to flourish. Any old place seemed to do.

A bank made by a bulldozer when leveling for the house seemed to be the ideal location for these sun-loving plants, even though it was unpromising red clay. I proceeded to forage and transplant such things as day flowers with their blue blossoms, magenta mullein pinks with gray leaves, ox-eyed daisies, purplish-pink phlox, a few wild roses, trailing sweet peas, some wild orange day lilies, and white boneset, plus a few lesser known plants that I had to identify in botany books.

In the midst of this project, the vegetable garden demanded my attention. All gardeners know one does not plant and cultivate according to personal schedules but with consideration of temperature, moisture, and phases of the moon. Thus I was busy for weeks and shamefully neglected the newly planted bank.

To my astonishment, I found that the wild plants had thrived on neglect. They liked it. For centuries they had been fending for themselves, becoming independent of fertilizers and extra watering. Thus, in spite of having been treated like stepchildren, the plants on the bank flourished and, over the years, became a mini-jungle. Periwinkle spread into a mat, poison ivy insinuated itself when my back was turned, a few ferns showed up from somewhere, and, lo, in the first weeks of June and continuing throughout the summer, I enjoy a riot of colors scattered over the bank in combinations that no decorator would tolerate but nature encourages.

That bank had not been intended so much for a floral display as for collecting these low-rated flowers to show their great number and variety as well as their intrinsic beauty. From time to time I crowded in new specimens such as the dainty yellow baptisia, a pink my neighbors call "kissies," orange butterfly weed, red fire pink, bee balm, and mountain mint. Even so, I have only a fraction of our indigenous plants. When one kind stops blooming, another is "buddin' to bloom," as our mountain boys say.

After watching individual blooming habits, I have transplanted certain wild plants into the "tame" garden. The pure yellow sundrop and the tall blue bellflower have been great additions, easing their way into the society of shasta daisies, foxgloves, snapdragons, and prized phlox. Today, according to my grandmother's estimate of society, the "bottom rail's on top." Democracy in the garden!

It is a daily pleasure to walk or drive the mile to the post office because our unpaved road is bordered by fence rows that provide a constant succession of wild flowers in a crazy-quilt jumble. When honeysuckle is in bloom, the air is filled with heavenly sweetness. The thickets are a breeding ground for young rabbits, who make their first excursions onto the open road and scurry home at the first sound of a car, as no doubt mama-rabbit has instructed them. A quail family often crosses from one side to the other with the mother in the lead and the father bringing up the rear and shooing the offspring when he becomes aware of human presence.

Our road is so little traveled that we are blessed by the absence of county workers with sprays, mowers, and swinging blades whacking at everything within reach. For years I have been gathering Queen Anne's lace, thistles, goldenrod, and blue and white asters on my way home. The number of plants from which to choose seems to rival the figures of the national debt, and I never feel guilty in gathering a bouquet for the house.

Recently, however, my attention was rudely awakened by a guest, who, after admiring my "country arrangement," asked, "Did you pick these along the road? You know there's a law. . . ."

That started me thinking, especially since I had long had my eye on a patch of white Siberian iris that had seeded themselves and multiplied in a very deep ditch where nobody but me (so I thought) could see them. I had planned to get a boy to dig some for me, but realized that perhaps I should get permission since they were along a main thoroughfare.

My visit to the office of the Highway Department was both amusing and informative. I decided I would act a slightly addled old lady, with hopefully enough wheedling charm to get around official pronouncements—a role not too hard to slip into. I was pleased when the young officer behind the desk rose to acknowledge my introduction. Good manners, I thought, that boded well for the interview.

"I was wondering," I began, "if I might dig some iris that are growing so deep in a ditch no one can see to enjoy them. The mowers cut them down regularly. I thought I'd better ask for permission since there might be a law. . . ."

"Yes, ma'am," said the young officer emphatically, "there *is* a law and this is what it says." He then recited a long, legally phrased enactment in which citizens are forbidden from molesting public property.

"But I won't be *molesting*," I objected, "I will be rescuing those poor iris." Then forgetting my assumed role, I launched into an ecological lecture on the damage being done by mowers and spraying and cited statistics on how many wild flowers had become extinct in recent years and ended by quoting a sentence I had read about the wild flower we save today perhaps being the cancer cure of tomorrow.

"Lady," said the young man in a stern voice but with an undisguised twinkle in his eye, "It would please me mightily to catch you digging those iris. I'd take your picture and have it printed in the local paper to show how a flower-lover, who should be setting a good example, was breaking the law. Don't you see we can't grant special favors. The law applies to everyone equally."

My only response was a question: "What harm does it really do for me to pick a few asters or joe-pye along our lane? I take them home, arrange them in vases where they give me and my guests pleasure. The absence of those few flowers cannot be noticed. And when I dig, I observe the Indian rule of passing up plant number one and plant number two and taking number three. Surely you wouldn't object to that?"

He shook his head. "You're rationalizing." (That remark made me suspect he had been to college.) "How would it be if *everybody* helped themselves to what they wanted? We can't have people disregarding regulations which are made for the good of the whole."

I recognized he had all the arguments and authority on his side and knew it was useless to continue, but asked: "Have you ever arrested anyone caught picking flowers along the highway?"

"No," he replied, "but if we see someone picking or digging, either along the road or in state parks, we stop and inform them of the law and ask their cooperation."

I felt chastened as he dismissed me with a grin, "I hope you will start setting a good example."

My! What an onus he was laying on my shoulders at this time of life. But, of course, he was right.

As I returned home along my country lane, I looked with mixed emotions at the mass of vegetation on either side. I could never again have the innocent pleasure of snipping at random. I could not be sure I would *never* yield to temptation, but if I picked a flower, I would carry a sense of guilt that would tarnish my pleasure.

I love the natural beauty of this lane, especially in September's golden glory—so different from modern manicured expressways. I am told that these weedy composites outnumber useful plants, and I believe it. They are mainly native, although some like the daisy, dandelion, and thistle come from Europe.

The story is told that after the fateful battle of Culloden (1746), a shipload of Scots landed in Baltimore and emptied their sodden mattresses, which had been filled with thistle down. They refilled with straw, and the discarded thistles took off, finding this country more congenial than their native Scotland, and at length spread to every state on the continent.

Toward the end of August, when dogwoods and sumac herald the approach of autumn with their bright red and yellow leaves, there begins a spectacular show by the composites—the category of plants considered to have reached the highest level in plant evolution. This group includes the brilliantly yellow sunflowers, all the blue and white asters, the various goldenrods, white boneset, and many others. Their flowers grow in clusters, arranged for mutual benefit, and each has developed its own mechanism to attract insects to ensure pollination. Their seeds are said to "ride, cling, and float." Ragweed seeds, for instance, are spread by the wind. Some seeds stick to the coats of animals, and some are disseminated by birds. The number of seeds from composites alone would tax the largest computer.

On the way to the village there is a twenty-acre field where cabbages were gathered in early September. In less than a month's time, the entire field took on a rosy hue, and when I stopped to investigate, I found every inch of that huge field covered with the lovely pink seedlike blossoms of lady's thumb. Fast work. The words for composites are *ubiquitous* and *invincible*.

I was driving down the lane in late September with a friend who pointed to a tall stalk with yellow flowers like a candelabrum and asked its name. I did not know whether she was testing my knowledge or merely asking a question in the manner of children, who do not necessarily want an answer but are showing their awareness. If I had told her it was yellow wingstem (*Verbesina occidentalia*), she would have accused me of showing off and would most likely have forgotten the name anyway, so I played it safe and answered, "Just one of the composites."

I am faced with a dilemma. Where am I to get all the flowers I need for the house now that I must be "an example"? From my own bank, of course, and from neighbors' yards. I am fortunate to live among friendly mountain people. When I visit Bessie, Vera, or Ida, I am always urged to *"pick yourself a flower pot."* That expression must be strictly local as I have never run across it elsewhere. It simply means to gather a bunch of flowers at will for a vase at home. I hope some of the next generations pass this idiom down to their children so that the quaint invitation will not be lost like some of our wild flowers.

Energy for the Eighties

On my eightieth birthday no reporter asked for my recipe for longevity. If he had, he certainly would not have printed anything so silly. No one would believe a sensible octogenarian could be serious about such a ridiculous prescription for vibrant health. Nevertheless, freedom from aches and pains at my advanced age impels me to risk being laughed at as I publish my secret.

Where anyone can see me I am the archetype of a proper grandmother, but in the seclusion of my bedroom I indulge in a personalized brand of exercise, and always comfortably in bed.

I loathe calisthenics. I detested enforced gym in school. Cavorting in a crowd has never been any fun for me. I enjoy gardening because there is something to show for the digging, stooping, and lifting, but swinging arms and legs and twisting the torso is an intolerable bore.

However, years of observation have convinced me that some exercise is vital if one is to remain limber and reasonably acceptable in appearance. My solution gives me double benefit because I can't help laughing at myself, and laughter as an aid to health has recently been popularized by no less eminent a critic and author than Norman Cousins. I have no way of determining which does more good, my method of exercise or the laughter. Perhaps it takes both.

creek named for her. The later Betty may have been a descendant.

Another neighbor showed me a spring on the Zack Dillard land where Indians had come from time immemorial to get water and continued to do so as long as they remained in the neighborhood. Half a mile to the north, where Estatoah Falls sends its water splashing into a small creek that empties into the river, the Grist family, longtime land owners, say that pottery and arrowheads turn up even today when the fields are plowed—positive evidence that this was Indian country.

These Indians were Cherokees of Iroquoian stock. Exactly when they migrated south is not known, but DeSoto, in 1540, found them well established. In 1746 James Glen, Royal Governor in Charles Town, wrote that they were the largest southern Indian group, numbering 20,000 (probably an exaggeration) and capable of putting 2,300 warriors into battle. They occupied a territory of 118,000 square miles, equal to the combined area of the New England states plus New York, most of it mountains.

The Cherokees, all kin and loosely federated, were divided into three nations: Overhills, Middle, and Lower. Those of this area, i.e., North Georgia, western North Carolina, and Piedmont South Carolina, were the Lower Cherokees, occupying only one-fourth of the territory.

The first accounts written about this country described streams teeming with fish and game plentiful, including buffalo and deer. Gigantic trees of the virgin forest stood well apart. The woodman's ax of later years changed this and produced second- and third-growth thickets. In addition to wild game there were some domestic hogs and cattle, escapees from the Spanish expedition. Passenger pigeons were so numerous they were said to have darkened the skies. The earliest writers referred to this section as the Cherokee Mountains.

In the beginning, the Indians were on reasonably good terms with the English because they wanted trade goods, arms, and ammunition, while the English sought the furs and pelts the Indians could provide. The first white men who ventured into the territory were fur traders. It was when settlers began to infiltrate that trouble began.

History is most often written as power conflicts. Wars are punctuation marks. The Cherokee War, as it is called, was in reality a part of the larger French and Indian War, which was centered chiefly on the English gaining control of Canada and the Mississippi River from the French. The Cherokee War has been glossed over with brief comment or entirely omitted from most history books, and few people today are aware that it ever took place. And yet it is the one event, the only event in American history, in which this particular valley played a part. Because of that it seems worth reviewing for natives as well as newcomers. What took place here had far-reaching national significance, and the telling may stir imaginations and cause reflection.

The background leading to the English campaigns against the Indians in 1760 and 1761 is a sequence of meetings, broken treaties, hostages seized, and violence on both sides. As year after year tensions mounted, bloodshed became inevitable. At intervals the Indians had gone to Charles Town to confer with royal governors, all of whom save Governor Bull, who was deemed too "soft" with the Indians, were contemptuous of the "savages" and treated them as inferiors. Headmen of the tribes were given only minimum respect, and the slightest excuse was used to grab hostages.

Actual war can be said to have begun when Colonel Archibald Montgomery and his men were sent by ship to Charles Town from New York, where they were attached to British forces fighting the French in Canada. On landing, they were joined by South Carolina Militia and Rangers and immediately began their march toward the mountains. After several stops, they arrived at Fort Prince George, a Piedmont fortification built much earlier in conjunction with the Cherokees, who feared their Choctaw and Chickasaw enemies and sought English aid and protection. It was situated across the Keowee River from the Indian town with the same name. On June 23, 1760, the English crossed the river, burned or destroyed every Indian town they passed through, and marched on to spend the night at Oconee Old Fields. They proceeded west over the well-traveled Warwoman Road, now a main thoroughfare into Clayton, Georgia. At that point they turned north into the valley about which I am now writing.

In those days, so we have been told, there were no roads as such, only paths, first made by animals, then followed by Indians until definite trails were established. I find it hard to imagine the Redcoats and Highlanders in their fine uniforms and kilts, accompanied by their pipers, marching in formation in such a wild country. I marvel they made any progress at all. In researching the period, my husband discovered he had a remote ancestor who marched as a foot soldier in the militia up this very valley, and later past the site on which we built our house.

The troops went into action sooner than they had expected, because five miles below the town of Etchoe the Rangers were attacked by the Indians as they entered a heavily wooded area known as Tessentee Old Town. An estimated six hundred Indians, hiding behind trees, in what today would be termed guerilla warfare, fell upon their enemy with arrows and bullets. Two English captains were killed. Confusion reigned. Only the Highlanders did not panic and in time drove the Indians from their cover, and the battle was over. The English counted seventeen dead and sixty-six wounded. They marched into the then-deserted town of Etchoe, where the troops rested.

Montgomery took stock of the situation. He was in rugged mountain country, sixty miles from base, burdened with a large number of wounded, and subject to surprise attack. He had been ordered to return at the earliest possible moment to join General Amherst in the siege and reduction of Montreal. With these facts in mind, he decided to return posthaste to Fort Prince George, which he reached on July 1. Here he left the wounded and six months' supplies and headed down the path to his waiting ships. He left behind him a nation of hostile Indians, who reasoned that the British forces feared them, as evidenced by their hasty withdrawal, and were thus emboldened to continue their harassment of white settlers. And so the campaign ended with Montgomery winning a battle but losing a campaign and settling nothing.

No event is solitary. In retrospect, we easily see that every happening is connected with what is taking place simultaneously. Such was the case in this conflict when Fort Loudon, near present-day Knoxville, Tennessee, a fort built largely by Virginians, was under siege by the Overhills, who had turned against the English. The troops inside, near starvation, raised a white flag and agreed to surrender the fort, and the Indians pledged that the garrison would be allowed to march to Fort Prince George unmolested. The fort was then evacuated, but the Indians, in violation of their pledge, fell upon the soldiers, scalping, killing, and taking prisoners. All officers were killed save one. With this massacre, the Indians exulted that they had avenged their sufferings at the hands of the English over the years.

When the news of the fall of Fort Loudon reached the Lower Cherokees, they in turn besieged Fort Prince George, demanding its surrender likewise. Charles Town ordered Captain Milne to "hold the fort," but he wrote back, "The Cherokees have blockaded us up like a parcel of cattle for the slaughter."

Peace overtures were begun by both Virginia and South Carolina, and in time the Indians lifted their siege. Their change of heart was due entirely to their need for supplies and trade goods. The French, their allies, had promised much but delivered little or nothing. The warlike Overhill chief, Oconostata himself, led a delegation to Keowee to discuss terms with other Cherokees. Necessity had forced him to resume relations with the hated English. He even permitted barter of food for the fort.

However, peace was more remote than ever, for South Carolina was so enraged at the Fort Loudon massacre that it determined to "reduce the Cherokees to a state of subjugation."

Although the French had come down from Illinois with more promises of aid and whipped up the Overhills into warlike frenzy, the pinch from a lack of supplies, especially salt, cooled their ardor for war. With winter coming on, the disgruntled braves returned to their villages. The English went into winter quarters.

The early months of 1761 were uneasy on both sides. The Indians were reduced to rags. South Carolina did send a fair amount of goods as well as a welcome change of command at Fort Prince George, which eased the tension temporarily, so that better relations prevailed from March until May and caused the Indians to release 113 prisoners, holding back only a few to secure release of Cherokees held by the English.

There were moments that spring when war seemed avoidable, but peace talk was not popular in Charles Town. The Colony considered it had suffered too much, and the Crown waited for better weather and adequate forage for livestock to launch a new expedition, the plans for which were already in the making.

By late May, Colonel James Grant, with British Regulars, South Carolina Militia and Rangers, plus friendly Indians to act as scouts, was marching "up the path" in a determined assault against the Cherokee Nation. Lord Amherst, angered at the breach of terms at Fort Loudon, gave orders that the Cherokees be punished in such a way as to prevent "all further outrages and encroachments." He commanded Colonel Grant to "chastize [sic] and reduce them to absolute necessity of suing for peace."

Grant's army consisted of 2,828 officers and men and stretched out two miles in the march. They followed the same route taken by Montgomery the year before and, on June 9, bivouacked at Estatoah Old Field, seventeen miles south of Etchoe, probably in the vicinity of Rabun Gap and Dillard, Georgia.

I have walked with a group of historians, books and maps in hand, attempting to identify the spots where action took place so long ago. This is a difficult task. Mileage estimates varied, and in those days, few details were given in early accounts. It takes imagination to see back of present-day paved roads, modern motels, craft shops, and eating places to a time when there was nothing here but woods, wildlife, and an occasional Indian village.

The experts agree, however, on the spot where the initial and decisive battle took place. The rear guard of the English was fired upon by the Indians close to where Mulberry Road runs into Highway 441, at a place called Tryphosa. A large band of Indians was massed to one side. Light infantry quickly turned to face the Indians on the slopes. Grant forded a stream and formed his battle line on open ground.

I never drive past that curve in the road without trying to visualize what took place and ponder why it had to happen. For it did happen, and suddenly. The English quickly gained control, and the Indians never again made a frontal attack. Ten British soldiers were killed and fifty-three wounded. Indian losses were not recorded. Grant marched into the heart of Indian country unopposed.

The rest of the story is one of burning town after town, with such Indian names as Joree, Cowee, Ussauch, Steco, Watauga. Grant marched on, stopping at Nequassee and using its large domed house as a hospital. Detachments were sent out to destroy corn and pea vines and to cut down peach trees. Watauga, a town of fifty houses, was put to the torch. They did not burn Cowee, the largest of the Middle settlements, but kept it as a base of operations. All the towns were deserted on their arrival.

31

The women and children had fled to the woods, and the men had gone to join the Overhills.

After these disasters the Cherokees, being near starvation and surrounded by the enemy, were forced to sue for peace. The Little Carpenter, Attaculla, a truly noble and intelligent chief, went first to Virginia but was shuttled off to South Carolina. The great Oconostata sent a brave called "Old Caesar" to Grant with the pitiful picture of starvation and death among the women and children hiding in the hills. Grant was said to have been genuinely moved, but he had to present the terms worked out in Charles Town, which were:

1. Both sides were to return all prisoners.
2. Cherokees were to return all stolen livestock. (Impossible because it had all been eaten.)
3. English sovereignty was to be recognized, and the Little Carpenter was to be the emperor of the Cherokee Nation.
4. The Cherokees were to make peace with the Catawbas and Chickasaws.
5. English trade was to resume.
6. One or two braves from each region must be delivered to be put to death.

Grant, it is claimed, tried to make the treaty as lenient as possible. After much bickering, the treaty groups met at Ashley Falls since there was smallpox in Charles Town. Demands for the delivery of Indian braves for execution were dropped, but the Lower Cherokees were compelled to cede half their hunting grounds. The Little Carpenter agreed to the terms and headed back to present them to his people. Grant then departed with his men.

In early December the Little Carpenter with a "second string" of representatives arrived in Charles

Town to hold a last conference there. The Overhills had not signed this pact; they made their own treaty with Virginia. A footnote to this Charles Town meeting tells of trade goods being offered to the needy Indians of such shabby quality that they were politely refused. The Indians did, however, beg for and get ammunition for hunting, but lingered so long on the bounty of the Colony that they were not-so-politely asked to go home.

Sociologists write about such conflicts from a different angle. They show two unequal cultures in conflict and, as repeated often in history, the more advanced civilization with technical knowledge inevitably overpowering the more primitive peoples.

Today's ecologists take still another stand and praise the harmony that existed between the Indian and his environment and his reverent treatment of tree, plant, and land. They contrast that with what the white man has done for his own gratification and to the detriment of the planet.

Doubtless, our national thinking has evolved and changed radically since the days when the English troops used the burned-earth tactic against the Indian villages. Today we read with a sense of guilt, but it must be remembered that the mind-set of that day was vastly different. Consider how a white settler felt when he returned home to find his cabin burned, his wife and children scalped, killed, or taken prisoner. He would not have taken into consideration that royal governors had seized hostages, broken treaties, and treated the Indians as inferiors. His vengeance would be based on hatred of the feared "savages."

In colonial America, Europeans seemed to feel nothing wrong with the appropriation of a less populated land. Spain set the example, but it wanted gold and treasure, whereas England needed land, and the New World seemed theirs for the taking. It is doubtful that anyone considered it morally wrong to dispossess the red man of his homeland. Today we acknowledge our guilt and feel our reparation inadequate.

The postscript to the Cherokee War, which broke the Cherokees' spirit so that they never again made a concerted attack, came seventy-five years later, when President Andrew Jackson ordered their forceful removal to Oklahoma. There is no greater blot on American history than what is known as the Trail of Tears. There is, however, a local story that somewhat mitigates our feeling of shame and may help to shake off some of its sobering effects.

When soldiers were rounding up the Cherokees for deportation to Oklahoma, several Indian families fled and hid in a cave on the side of that massive mountain that goes by the name of Pickens' Nose.* In time, two white men learned of their presence, probably while rounding up their hogs and cattle that had been turned out to graze in the forest. Taking pity on the plight of the refugees, the Hopper and Williams families supplied grain and other necessities over a period of several years, or until it was legally safe for the Indians to appear in public. The Indians, of course, were able to get game and

---

*Local legend describes how this unusually massive mountain was given the name of Pickens' Nose. Andrew Pickens, one of South Carolina's Revolutionary generals, was a young officer in the early expeditions against the Indians. On a march, his men caught view of the mountain's profile in the distance and joked about its resemblance to their leader's Roman nose. In spite of time and weather, it is still a noble proboscis.

some wild plants, but they were literally kept alive by the generosity of those two families for whom it must have been a sacrifice, since those were not days of abundance. Their descendants tell the story with justifiable pride.

I have visited that cave twice with members of the Georgia Botanical Society and am convinced it would be foolhardy to try to find it without a competent guide. One must travel many miles on a government road and hike a half mile around the mountain. There is no distinguishable path. One climbs over and under fallen trees, scales slippery rocks, and tramps through deep fallen leaves, thick with the smell of damp woods.

My second trip was on a cold, windy day in the fall of 1982. Gigantic icicles hung from north-facing rocks, but the sun was shining. I followed close on the heels of the leader, and we were soon far ahead of the crowd—mostly city folk. Our hike ended in a short but steep climb to boulders marking the entrance to the cave. Without previous knowledge, no one would suspect a great underground cavity lying concealed below.

When the leader went into the cave to inspect, I was on a high promontory with a view so vast, so majestic, that I was humbled before its beauty. In the flash of that moment I knew how the Cherokees had felt. These mountains were not just a place to live; they were a part of the Indians' very lives, their bloodstreams, woven into the fabric of their bodies, built into their bones, and alive in their consciousness. I knew why the Indians were willing to risk starvation rather than be parted from them. Unconsciously I raised my arms above my head in a gesture that expressed feelings I could not put into words.

The rest of the party came puffing up. The guide gave a brief talk, and we all descended into the rocky cavern. At the bottom a young girl gave an excited shriek when her shoe dug up a piece of broken pottery. Tangible evidence helps some people believe.

A geologist in the group explained that this was not a true cave, though it had served that purpose for the hunted Indians. He stretched our imaginations when he said those enormous rocks had come into existence in the Precambrian Age—some seven hundred to eight hundred million years ago. Later, when continents were colliding, the granite rocks had been pushed up toward the surface. The last recorded upheaval was a mere hundred million years ago in the Cretaceous Period, and it was probably then that the huge slabs broke apart, one tilting over the other to roof it. A narrow slit across the top allowed air and light to penetrate, but now rhododendrons screened it from view.

There was a stream at the bottom for which, no doubt, the Indians gave thanks to the Great Spirit. The shadowy cave, shielded from the wind, was comfortably warm. The rock walls were still colored by the smoke of long ago. Life in such a place would not have been easy. I could not imagine myself or anyone I know evincing the fortitude of those hiding Indians.

We climbed back into the sunshine, and I was again face to face with that expanse of mighty mountains. The Indians were long since departed, but I turned homeward with the certainty that their Great Spirit hovered over their hiding place and still guarded their mountains.

So Often Bread Is Taken for Granted

Bread is basic. Baking bread is an art, as creative as painting a picture, shaping a jug, or weaving a tapestry, and probably more appreciated by the family. A browned loaf fresh from the oven lifts one's self-esteem as little else can. It satisfies a deep feminine instinct for nesting.

Shortly after retiring to the country, I began to bake my own bread—not because homemade bread is superior in taste to bread from the grocery or because it is more nutritious or even because it is more economical, of which I am doubtful, or, in fact, for any noble reason. I measure, stir, knead, and keep on kneading, let rise, punch down, let rise again, and bake from a sense of guilt. My first loaf was an act of penance.

In my heady enthusiasm over embracing a bucolic life-style, I jumped at a neighbor's invitation to attend an auction of household goods at a farm where she was sure there would be authentic antiques. She recited the items she remembered, among them a wooden tray for mixing bread. I had seen such articles, probably copies, in the city, filled with fruit, pinecones, or Christmas balls, and I thought one might look charming on my pine table. At the last moment, when I was unable to go with her, I commissioned her to bid on the wooden bowl for me.

Next morning her daughter appeared with the coveted bowl in hand.

"Mama says she hopes this is what you wanted."

"Oh, yes," I replied enthusiastically, even though the big hand-hewn tray was gray with age and hardly an object of beauty.

The girl continued, "Mama says a dealer from the city kept bidding but you told her to get it, so she did."

"Fine," I beamed. "And what was it finally knocked down for?"

"Forty-six dollars," she replied.

F O R T Y - S I X   D O L L A R S !

I had expected ten, or fifteen at the most, for this was before inflation had started its dizzy spiral. To hide my dismay I hurried for my checkbook. There was nothing to do but pay the forty-six dollars I could ill afford at that time. I held out the check with somewhat less than enthusiastic thanks and carried my crown jewels into the kitchen.

The well-worn wood confirmed that it was a genuine antique, although it was impossible to know from what kind of tree it had been made. Only an expert could identify it as oak, maple, cherry, or pine, but it must have been a noble tree to allow for the carving of this oversize (24″ x 14″) mixing bowl with rounded corners. It was much too large for my pine table, and as I contemplated it, I kept thinking how many war orphans that money might have fed, or how that amount would have helped toward next winter's wood supply. How could I have been so stupid? Why hadn't I given my neighbor a figure at which to stop bidding? I didn't know whether to laugh or cry, so I did the human thing and took out my frustration on the innocent object.

"I'm going to put you to work," I addressed my wooden monster as I gave it a thorough scrubbing at the sink. "I'm going to make you pay for being so valuable."

I rolled up my sleeves, got out a cookbook, and went to work immediately. To my amazement, I discovered that baking bread was fun. From that moment, bread-making burgeoned into a passion.

Through the country grapevine, the news of my extravagance leaked out, and I was bombarded with recipes for bread. I tried them all, using my new treasure, of which I was becoming inordinately proud as it took on a pleasing patina with repeated use. The recipe that seemed most appropriate for my venerable antique is named Early Colonial Bread, and it remains my favorite. (See recipe on page 42.)

Having become somewhat cocky through the luck of a beginner, I then proceeded to make a series of failures: horrible, heavy, indigestible messes, which I tried to blame on this and that, but the stern fact finally penetrated that making bread is not a game or casual pastime, but an art, and like other arts, demands the discipline of following established and proven practices. The five-finger exercises of bread-making, I learned, include exact measurements, careful temperature control, and a detailed following of directions. Only after these are mastered might one indulge in alterations.

Cookbooks abound with good recipes for bread, but they do not spell out the mystique that transforms a kitchen chore into an experience of wonder. This, I found, comes with the intimacy of much handling. The *feel* of the dough sends a message to my brain, and I note the difference due to different grains, to changes taking place as the various ingredients work together during the kneading. I sense something wonderful taking place. I was quick to realize that yeast, a living organism, is the prima donna responsible for the success of the show, and that like most leading ladies, she must have things to suit her: the right temperature, just enough sugar but not too much, some salt to inhibit too-quick action. In its own good time, yeast is responsible for turning sugar into alcohol and carbon dioxide, which aerate the dough and, with the aid of shortening, adds lightness. Experienced cooks had already discovered all this and coded their findings into recipes. Therefore, it is only intelligent to follow a recipe *exactly.*

My weekly baking sessions produced two unexpected bonuses: old memories and new friends. The smell of baking bread brought back my childhood, when I thought that the *smell* in our kitchen was better than the "lightbread" our cook made every Saturday. That I considered not half so good as the soft, cottony, store-bought five-cent loaf I sometimes ate at friends' houses. On our farm we ate a lot of cornbread, but all other bread was made of white flour: batter cakes and waffles for breakfast, beaten biscuits for company, biscuits or yeast rolls for evening dinner. The flour came in a huge barrel, and we children deliberately ate more than the usual amount of bread as the flour got down toward the bottom because we coveted the barrel for our favorite sport.

Country children invent their own pastimes, not having the ready-made entertainments of the city. We would take the empty flour barrel, washed and dried, to the front terrace, boost a child into it, with a pillow back of the head, lay the barrel on its side, and give a big push over the terrace, which had a three-foot drop. The barrel would gain speed and roll about twenty-five feet out onto the lawn, giving the adventurous soul a dizzy spin. We clamored for our turn and thought it our best sport.

As for new friends, I discovered a camaraderie among home bakers. I was being "accepted"—like being asked to join the Junior League. There was, of course, no organization, but as individuals they all assumed an unspoken, but definite superiority over their friends who bought their bread at the store. I too was smug, feeling like the good house-wife in Proverbs whose price "is above rubies and who eateth not the bread of idleness."

With habitual baking, it became obvious that I could not consume all the bread I baked, and I joyfully distributed it among my friends. One kind gentleman, the recipient of a hand-out warm from the oven, mailed me a poem which he insisted was signed "Anon." A framed copy now hangs on my kitchen wall and reads:

> Be careful when you touch bread.
> Let it not lie uncared for—unwanted.
> So often bread is taken for granted.
> There is so much beauty in bread:
> Beauty of sun and soil,
> Beauty of patient toil.
> Winds and rain have caressed it,
> Christ often blessed it.
> Be gentle when you touch bread.

Those lines were the needed antidote to my pride. I now feel humble. Each loaf is a miracle and I am a part of this joint achievement. As my mind marches along these lines, I smile to think that such a homely act as making bread has given me an insight into a basic truth.

Early Colonial Bread

1/2 cup cornmeal
1 tablespoon salt
1/4 cup cooking oil or shortening
1/3 cup brown sugar
  or 3 tablespoons molasses
  or honey
2 cups boiling water
2 packages or 2 tablespoons dry active yeast
1/2 cup lukewarm water
3/4 cup whole wheat flour
1/2 cup rye flour
4 1/2 to 5 cups unbleached white flour

Combine the cornmeal, salt, oil or shortening, brown sugar (or molasses or honey) in a large mixing bowl. Add boiling water, stir, and let cool. Dissolve the dry active yeast in the lukewarm water. Add this yeast mixture to the cornmeal mixture after it has cooled.

With a large wooden spoon, stir in the whole wheat, rye, and unbleached white flours. Turn out onto a floured surface and knead for 8 to 10 minutes, adding additional flour when necessary. Place in a greased bowl, cover, and let rise in a warm place until double. Punch down and divide into 2 loaves. Let rise 10 minutes. Place each loaf in a greased loaf pan, cover, and let rise until *almost* double. Bake in a preheated 350-degree oven for 45 to 50 minutes. Turn out onto a wire rack. Admire and enjoy! Yields 2 loaves.

The method used in the following recipe is different from the usual procedure. Dry yeast is sprinkled *on top of* the flour and the warm liquid poured over the whole. I have found this way to be quicker and just as satisfactory.

Honey Bread

1 cup white unbleached flour
1 1/2 cups whole wheat flour
1/2 cup rye flour
2 packages or 2 tablespoons dry active yeast
2 cups milk
1 tablespoon salt
3 tablespoons shortening
1/2 cup honey
2 1/2 cups white unbleached flour

Combine the white unbleached, whole wheat, and rye flours in a large mixing bowl. Sprinkle the dry active yeast on top. Combine the milk, salt, shortening, and honey in a medium saucepan over low heat and stir constantly until just warm.

Pour liquid mixture over dry mixture and beat with an electric mixer for 30 seconds at low speed, then 3 minutes at high speed or, if beating by hand, until gluten begins to form. Stir in 2 1/2 cups white flour to make a moderately stiff dough. Turn out onto a well-floured surface and knead for 8 to 10 minutes. Place in a greased bowl, cover, and let rise in a warm place until double. Punch down, let rest, cover, and let rise again. Bake in a preheated 350-degree oven for 35 to 40 minutes. Yields 2 loaves.

Life-Style Updated

T he first meeting of the Last Chance Co-op was being held, and I was invited. "Why Last Chance?" I queried the organizer, a newcomer with two master's degrees and one Ph.D., a pretty Phi Beta Kappa wife, and some original ideas on simplified living.

"You may read anything into it you like." He laughed. "But it is the actual name of a tiny school building out Betty Creek Road, which some old-timers remember attending. It is now a delapidated shack near where we shall be meeting. It's as good a name as any."

The co-op has grown to forty-five members, about twenty-five of whom regularly attend the monthly potluck supper—strong on health foods, sprouts, homemade whole wheat bread, and the like—and spend the evening going through the wholesaler's catalog and placing orders. The leader calls out, "We have to get a twenty-five-pound sack of rolled oats. Who wants rolled oats?" Members shout their orders, taking more or less to meet requirements. The grocery list includes juices, oils, grains and flour, nuts, cheese, dried fruits, and many health foods not on most store shelves. The orders mount up. In a week, volunteers will meet the truck, then package and price the orders to be picked up.

This group is not unique. Food co-ops are burgeoning all over the country. All the members are relative newcomers; only one has roots in the mountains. They seem to be middle class or upper middle class. Most have a college education, with a sprinkling of higher degrees. Only two couples are retired, the majority being young or middle-aged, and quite a few are divorced. There is no ethnic, religious, or cultural bond. What, then, cements them?

The quick answer is bulk buying of quality food at a savings, but that is only a part. The real significance is far deeper. The common denominator is a commitment to an emerging life-style—a trend by no means local. The co-op is incidental, an outgrowth of the main concern, but it can serve as a microcosm of an idea that is catching on nationwide. Duane Elgin's book calls it "Voluntary Simplicity."

Another *ism?* Not exactly. This differs from idealistic experiments of the past in having no one leader, no set rules, no communes, no well-defined code of conduct, and no missionary zeal. It is strictly personal. Each in his own good time chooses his own path, formulates his own creed; and how he puts it into practice is his own business. Sounds like possible anarchy, but it doesn't work out that way.

As I got to know this blue-jeaned crowd, with a good number of bearded men and long-haired women, I found them all extremely intelligent, well read, and friendly. They are, without exception, ecologically militant and politically disillusioned. Only a handful retain connection with organized religion. One seldom hears the word *God*, but some of His other names—Love, Creative Energy, and Light—are heard often in conversation.

They all grew up on Reich's *The Greening of America*, DuBose's *The God Within*, Schumacher's

Small is Beautiful, and Rachel Carson's *Silent Spring,* and other provocative analyses of the world's ills. They are convinced that our planet is speeding toward disaster unless trends are reversed. But they are equally convinced that life *can* be meaningful, fulfilling, and even beautiful and are out to make it so, at least for themselves. Each is hacking his way through the jungle of tradition, custom, and outworn practices—a road full of struggles and setbacks and one requiring a pioneering spirit. Each is intent on finding the way best for him, and this goal is leading them all by different paths toward voluntary simplicity.

It should be stated immediately that voluntary simplicity should not be equated with poverty, which in all but rare cases is *in*voluntary. Nor does it reject all technology and progress in an effort to "go back to nature" like Thoreau, or necessarily require a rural setting, although that does seem to make it easier. It is rather a balance between austerity and self-indulgence. It boils down to a point of view.

In his letter to the Galatians, St. Paul lists the fruits of the spirit as love, joy, peace, long-suffering, gentleness, goodness, meekness, and temperance. Some of the "fruits" of voluntary simplicity are

1. A shift in diet away from processed foods, and in some cases, from meat altogether.
2. Saving energy: burning wood when practical and using as little oil, etc., as possible.
3. Organic gardening; raising much of one's own food.
4. Buying only for actual need, with an eye for durability.
5. War on waste of any sort; recycling when possible.
6. Developing new skills; becoming self-sufficient.

7. Disposing of unused possessions and clutter.
8. Joining local efforts toward like ends; i.e., this co-op.
9. Concern for spiritual growth and the quality of life.

That list did not strike me as being particularly revolutionary. Thrift and frugality were practiced as well as preached in my youth and down through the Great Depression. I checked my own habits, and with the exception of energy saving, which was not a problem until recently, I can say that I have always acted from these precepts within the framework of my circumstances.

But I have witnessed a radical change in the thinking pattern of the entire nation. I recall a nephew, when he received a car for his eighteenth birthday, saying that a car was no longer a luxury, but a necessity. And from his point in time, he was right.

I think I know what happened. Technology following World War II caused industry to produce far more than we had formerly consumed. To meet the frantic needs of this manufacturing explosion, advertising stepped in with a deliberate campaign to make everyone think he *must* have a car, *must* have a better house than his parents, *must* also have a vacation house, or at least an expensive vacation, *must* discard last year's clothes to keep in style, and *must* have all the labor-saving devices that were flooding the market. All this on credit, which often backfired.

Eventually profligate spending began to be recognized as one of the causes of the stress that was corroding the spirit and begetting serious health problems. Waste, on a scale unknown in history, piled up. People were forced to do some serious

47

thinking. I was witnessing the result in the lives of individuals in the co-op. Self-sufficiency was their overall goal, and they were learning the hard lesson of being malleable in changing circumstances.

One city-bred man put it this way: "I no longer have to worry about losing my job or being forced to move, or really about anything that might happen. We are learning to cope. And the sense of freedom is worth all the *things* we used to think we must have."

What do these modern pioneers do to make a living? Again, an interesting diversity. For the most part, they are gainfully employed. They have created their own opportunities in a community without much to offer. Some joke about their simplified living not being entirely voluntary because of past financial entanglements. Hope sustains them.

One young couple, after years of tending an estate, is now homesteading on seventeen acres of their own land with a garden and animals. She creates imaginative unicorns, monkeys, and frogs, which are sought by prestigious city stores for use in window displays. He works in construction.

A medical doctor, his wife, and three children have lived in a remote area while he studied herbal and native remedies. Now, with the aid of a registered nurse, he delivers babies in the home; homebirth, it is called. He also holds a psychiatric clinic several days a week.

The founder of the co-op and his wife managed a farm for retarded adults with notable success. He is now teaching the use of computers and writing, while she pursues her career in astrology, gives lectures on ecological education, and serves as an officer in Friends of the Mountains.

An Agnes Scott graduate is a recognized potter, whose original earth-toned creations are snapped up at fairs. One girl works at *Foxfire*. One man inspects smokestacks to check compliance with the law. One has his own construction company. Two women in their sixties, longtime friends, bought thirty-seven acres and built separate homes, both homes heated with wood and with solar panels for heating water. They garden organically, raise sheep, goats, and guinea fowls. One lectures on no-tilling gardening, termed "Permaculture"; the other holds classes in basket weaving. Both are extremely active in their church, belong to Homemakers and an organic gardening club, are expert weavers and cooks. They even take honey from two hives of bees. And they still have time to entertain guests at meals and occasionally play bridge with friends.

If we revert to the simile of "fruits," we may well ask what kind of tree produces voluntary simplicity. What is the motivation? What sets off the photosynthesis?

The search for the meaning of life has become everyday talk. It is no longer left to philosophers in ivory towers. Scientists are supplying answers in language acceptable to modern thinking. Physics is giving explanations of the creation of the earth to clarify ancient myths. The exploration of the atom, once thought to be the base upon which all matter is formed, continues and has produced neutrons, protons, quarks, and other hypothetical entities that give rise to a challenging theory of a unified world—one in which every atom is unique and at the same time necessary to the whole. Translated into human life, these unique atoms combine to produce unique human beings—no two exactly alike, but all an intrinsic part of a pattern. Pursued further, this means that *what each person thinks, says, and does matters on a planetary scale.* Wow! What a burden to shoulder. But what a vision!

Old ideas are coming in new packaging. Truths that have lost their impact are being stated differently. Sectarian thinking may have to be jogged and rigid theologians pained, but they will find that these churchless people live by something remarkably like the Golden Rule. The global aspect—the thrust outward—keeps it from being entirely egocentric. I watch with interest from the vantage point of age and pray for understanding and tolerance.

I feel it only fair to ask, "Will such people make enough impact on society to change it significantly?"

One of the original co-op members, a retired corporation executive who is using his engineering training to design passive solar houses, was optimistic. He said, "Concern with today's problems is not local. It is an inescapable fact that we are moving into a global civilization. We *have to* broaden our horizons and *have to* assume responsibility for our planet. If we don't like the way the world is going, the first step is to change the direction of our own lives. The idea of streamlining one's life is spreading like wildfire, but since there is absolutely no organization, I can't give you statistics to prove its influence. There are books on the subject, like Marilyn Fergerson's *Aquarian Conspiracy*, that report what is actually taking place in various disciplines. If you watch TV or read magazines and newspapers, you'll be surprised how often these ideas are being tossed about."

He had talked around the subject, but he had not answered me directly, so I rephrased my question. "Can we expect these like-minded people to combine to create enough influence to reverse the trend toward chaos?"

He shook his head. "What will happen is different from anything in the past. You have to keep remembering that this is not a man-planned campaign. Joining up for a Big Push does not seem to be in the picture. The genius lies in vast numbers of individual efforts coming from many directions. What we are witness to is more like a mass of energy being generated for a quantum leap in the evolutionary process of man into a broader awareness. The energy is already in evidence. Such momentum cannot be stopped.

"Have you read the bestseller, *In Search of Excellence*? It is an eye-opener—an account of how twelve or more big corporations discovered and successfully applied a philosophy akin to what we have been talking about. Who would have expected big business to get into the act? Industry and technology have been considered the bad guys. Now we read they are putting value on the individual employee and giving him the responsibility for the success of the company. He is being made to feel that what he does is essential. This makes me think of the power in a tiny seed to crack a thick concrete sidewalk."

He ended by saying, "It's exciting . . . exciting to be a part of a decisive moment in history."

He's right. To watch this freewheeling, multi-option, yeasty experiment will be exciting. To be a part of it, even more so.

51

A Happy Birthday Letter to a Cousin's Husband

Dear Jan:
Congratulations on your sixty-fifth birthday! I am beaming you waves of affectionate good wishes along with this letter, which contains some gratuitous observations that I, being your senior by many years, hope you will read with due respect. Your wife writes that you are restless and suspects that it is because you do not welcome this milepost that points toward old age. How well I recall my sixty-fifth. Old? Not me. But later, when sober reason had stamped the reality of inevitable aging on my consciousness, I slumped into depression. "Attractive old age? No such thing. Old age is pathetic." What I dreaded most was the eventual loss of my faculties and my independence. But at that time good health made these fears seem so far off that, like Scarlett, I shoved them out of my mind to be taken care of "tomorrow."

Your masculine reaction will be different. Having been quite tall and handsome all your life, you hate the possibility of a slumped carriage, a bald head, or some disabling illness like arthritis, with its accompanying pain. (I have yet to meet a man who can take pain as women have had to.) I can almost hear you quoting Shakespeare, who always hits the nail on the head, and never more so than when he describes the seven ages of man, and ends, "His youthful hose, well sav'd, a world too wide / For his shrunk shank; and his big manly voice, / Turning again toward childish treble, pipes / And whistles in his sound." And then the gruesome finale, "Sans teeth, sans eyes, sans taste, sans everything." No one has ever painted a more devastating picture of old age. He speaks for all of us. But *must* he speak for all of us? Well, not for me anymore.

I remember reading Browning's "Rabbi Ben Ezra" for English Lit. "Grow old along with me! / The best is yet to be, / The last of life, for which the first was made." My comments then should not have been in a lady's vocabulary, but, so help me, I think he's right. I apologize.

It would be easy to go to a bookstore and mail you one of the books written on how to meet the aging process. There are hundreds, most of them excellent and based on the latest in medicine, psychology, and religion, but I disapprove of handing out tracts to bolster one's convictions. So bear with me while I fumble with words to refute Master Will's grim estimate. Pragmatist that I am, I searched until I found something that works . . . or, at least, softens the blows.

It took me years, a lot of tears, and many false starts to arrive at a plateau where I can survey the situation and accept it with equanimity. As proof of the latter, I am able to laugh, not cry, at my most recent passport picture, which could readily serve as model for that old *New Yorker* cartoon that read: "If you look like *that*, then you need the trip."

First I must bring up the subject of change, which is the key word in our historical period. Change in every phase of life has been accelerating at such a pace that we are bewildered and confused. There are books on this subject too, but the best metaphor

I know is the current popular sport of white-water rafting. You are in a raft with one or two others and a guide, each with an oar. The water is excitingly swift. You must think and act quickly to avoid the boulders that seem to be rushing upon you. With a little experience you can bypass the solid, immovable rocks, all the while racing with the water. Sometimes you don't quite make it, and a rock causes the raft to overturn, plunging you into the cold water—frightening for a second, but you retrieve your oar, climb back into the raft, and continue on your way. But as soon as one rock is safely past, another looms. Doesn't that sound like life and its problems? Those who have taken the trip come home with a better understanding of the rapidity of change and how to meet it. The secret is to flow with the stream rather than fight it.

This metaphor is the best I have found to cope with the steady march of the years, which brings wrinkles, an expanded waistline, white hair, and altered finances and neighborhoods. These disadvantages of growing old are beyond our control. This being the case, isn't it sensible to "flow with it" rather than expend energy on battles in a losing war? But how can we do this?

The answer sounds easy, but it is probably one of the hardest things an older person is asked to undertake, namely, to change thinking patterns.

This isn't a sermon on positive thinking, though that plays a part. I'm prescribing a shift from living in the past and glorifying it (a temptation for the elderly) and from worrying about the future and fearing its uncertainties. If we put our minds on what is happening at this very instant, we will find that something interesting is always taking place. For instance, at a meal, notice the taste of the bread, feel its texture; appreciate each vegetable's distinct contribution; give thanks (even orally, to the cook, your wife). Or when you are talking, look and listen to the person speaking to you, and you will hear much that he isn't putting into words. Or if you wake early and open the door, welcome the feel of the cool, damp air on your skin; strain your ears to hear the birds tuning up for the day. You will be rewarded, and you will find all your senses reactivated so that you feel, hear, taste, and smell with greater intensity. That in itself is a boon.

Give it a try. You won't understand until you do. Then, you will come to realize that NOW has a lot going for it. No matter how old you are, you will find that it isn't quite as bad as you anticipated. As the British would say, "It's really quite jolly."

We are meant to keep growing as long as we live, not physically, of course, but in understanding. When we stop growing, we've made a start at dying. We pass through many stages, and as we grow older, our values alter accordingly. I know mine have. I'll bet your idea of a pretty girl is conditioned by those luscious TV models. I, too, went through that stage, but now Rembrandt's *Portrait of an Old Woman* in the National Gallery in London is to me the most beautiful picture there.

One last relevant thought. At some time, every person must come to grips with physical death—his own or that of some member of the family or of a friend. Age sixty-five is as good a time as any to review what you have learned about the meaning of life and what you believe lies beyond. The great Jesuit priest and scientist, Teilhard de Chardin, voiced the hope that he would "die well." He didn't explain what he meant, but I think we all have the same wish. I have faith that if we live in the now, firmly pushing away any dread of the unknown future, in the end all will be "well." I hope you agree. Meanwhile, let's put our attention on *living* "well." Many, many happy returns.

Your elder cousin

What Shall I Bequeath to My Grandchildren?

Now that I am in my eighties, my mind resembles the ragbag that hung in the sewing room of my childhood home. With four girls to be dressed, that bag bulged with scraps of bright-colored ginghams, sturdy percales, stiff organdies, pretty dotted swiss, plain white cotton for panties and petticoats, and a few pieces of flowered silk, satin, and velvet from our eldest sister's party gowns.

My mind has accumulated a similar hodgepodge. Early memories: *Peter Rabbit* and *Squirrel Nutkin*, *Mother Goose*, and *A Child's Garden of Verses*. Grade school: the multiplication table and names of the capital cities of all forty-eight states. High school: a firm grounding in Latin, a smattering of French, some English grammar and composition, and my first taste of science in a chemistry lab. College: my introduction into the world of ideas—economics, sociology, history, psychology, philosophy, poetry and the arts. All these remembered studies may be compared to the sturdy materials for our school clothes. My one exciting year in the competitive business world, my marriage and the mothering of three sons, can only be compared to the choice velvet that we children stroked lovingly and laid aside as too fine to be cut up for doll clothes.

As years went by, my mind continued to expand and to absorb new ideas from books by great thinkers and also to gain its own wisdom from personal experience and travel. The current explosion of ideas from the world of science has given me a youthful thrill about the kind of world I live in. I can recall no ragbag scrap with which to compare this expanded consciousness, but my original analogy is strengthened by the fact that, as children, we drew from that assortment of scraps for making practically all our gifts. And I have come to the place in my life's journey where I am reaching back into the accumulation of the past to see what I have of value to bequeath to my grandchildren.

The times have ordained a new role for grandmothers who, like everyone else, are caught up in the vortex of change. I cannot possibly duplicate the part played by my beloved Virginia grandmother. As a tiny child I was her shadow during her four-month annual stay. With my chair as close to her rocker as I could get it, I turned pages of *Peter Rabbit* so that with her help as she looked down from her knitting, I was actually reading—so they tell me—at age three.

By osmosis I absorbed her code of conduct. I knew what was expected of me when, on leaving for a party, I was told to "mind your manners." That God was good and loving I took for granted because she had found it true. Her stories of the aftermath of the War Between the States made "Waste not, want not" and "Willful waste makes woeful want" basic truths that she had learned the hard way and indelibly engraved on my young mind. All this was possible because she was in our home long enough for casual talk to plant seeds for future growth.

Circumstances have made me an entirely different kind of grandmother. Because I live at a considerable distance from all ten grandchildren, I receive dutiful but brief visits with only enough time to learn what grade they are in, when the braces are expected to come off their teeth, what college they are aiming for, or what they want me to fix for lunch. My own independence has cost me the intimacy necessary for anything but surface talk.

I have already earmarked family possessions— silver, china, glass, and pictures—in most cases, objects they themselves have chosen. But since my own sense of values has altered, I long to give something more fundamentally useful, something I wish I had had at an earlier date, namely, a workable point of view. I would like to pass along to my descendants some ready talisman to be carried throughout their lives . . . something not exactly appropriate to be listed in a will.

No need to stress manners. Their mothers have done a good job there. At one time I thought a daughter-in-law a martinet, but her insistent demands produced four popular children—now adults—who are good company and welcomed everywhere because of their easy observance of the social amenities. Their father may have had a hand in this as he was brought up on the statement of a venerable South Carolina Negro, father of twelve, who told me: "When my chillun leave home, I tell 'em, 'Mind yo' manners, chillun, cause yo' manners'll take you where yo' money won't.'"

Nor is there any point in giving a lecture on the old-fashioned thrift of their ancestors, who waited for cash-in-hand before making a purchase, and who saved something, though it might be little, out of all income . . . practices my husband and I followed. But today's children must conform to current mores with mortgages and credit cards.

So I am choosing to pass on to my grandchildren two pieces of wisdom that have stood me in good stead. I cite these only as examples for I hope each will discover his own in due time. I have always liked maxims and proverbs—so straightforward and so easy to understand, although Mr. Einstein has taught us that what we have considered truths are only relatively so. Nevertheless, for all practical purposes, they have served me well.

My wise and loving father did not know his words would be filed in my memory along with those of Emerson, Shakespeare, Plato, and Benjamin Franklin. I distinctly recall the day we were driving into the city in a Model A Ford—he to business, I to high school in my senior year. It was early morning and the dew was sparkling on the blue-blue chickory blossoms alongside the road. I do not remember what we were discussing, but he said, "Never hesitate to explore a new idea." Then, after a pause, he added with that customary twinkle in his eyes, "But just don't go overboard."

He was probably unconscious of the perfect timing of his words. They became my battle cry as I rushed headlong into the knowledge that awaited me in a great northern college. My world exploded and expanded in courses in Bible history (then called Higher Criticism), in economics, sociology, history, chemistry, English literature, psychology, and philosophy. I am happy my father did not know how many times I *did* go overboard, since in my philosophy courses I was, in turn, a confirmed hedonist, stoic, nihilist, agnostic, or whatever I happened to be reading at the time. Perhaps his spirit helped me to surface and swim to solid ground. His advice, no doubt, conditioned the set of my brain. Later, however, I was to adopt a more sophisticated quotation from the Latin dramatist Terence: "Homo sum, humani nihil a me alienum puto," which in my loose translation reads: "I am a human and nothing pertaining to mankind is outside my interest."

A word of warning should be voiced here. Such an attitude is not for artists of any sort. They must maintain a steady, single focus and must jealously center on their dream, excluding all other interests. But I am not an artist, and diversified interests have provided me with a rich and interesting life, free of boredom and full of joy.

Recently, a grandson in college teased me by asking, "What are you up to now, Grandmother?" I was pleased to be able to reply, "I have just paid for an afternoon of private instruction on how to operate a computer." I remain faithful to my father's advice and find it worth passing on to my descendants.

At a much later date, after my husband's death, when time became blurred or altogether lost and I was desperately trying to find some meaning in my life, I was listening to a youth choir singing Christmas carols.

God rest you merry, gentlemen,
Let nothing you dismay.

That second line hit me like a rope thrown to a drowning man. "Let nothing you dismay." *Nothing?* Not the loss of my husband, not my daily worries, not growing old, not what might happen in the future? Nothing? "Yes," came the answer, *"nothing."* I grabbed at the possibility. How splendid it would be to be able to act from such a premise. Here were words to hold on to—words of reassurance and hope. "Let *nothing* you dismay." That line became my ritual. I repeated it when I lost valuable papers, misplaced car keys, forgot a family birthday, or watched a glorious sunset . . . alone.

But almost immediately it became apparent that there was a catch in it. Merely saying the line was not enough to make it always effective. The next two lines of the carol were necessary to make it "work":

> Remember Christ our Saviour
> Was born on Christmas Day.

In that fact lay the power.

I would be doing a disservice to my grandchildren if I did not here give a clue to my thinking because, taken alone, "Let nothing you dismay" could easily lead to a casual dismissal of trouble with a shrug. "So what?" "I don't care." "What's that to me?" "What difference will it make in the long run?" That is not what I wish to convey. Just the opposite. I was reaching out for a way to cope with troubles.

Though the words of the Christmas carol had caught my attention, I found that I was not able to put them into practice in *every* adverse circumstance. I was still impatient at standing in lines, I worried about my grown sons' decisions, I was distraught over environmental disasters. My own willpower was not enough to meet such problems with equanimity—without dismay.

In such a dilemma, where does one turn? To God, of course. But who is God, what is God, where is God? Everyone asks such questions sooner or later. They form the basis on which both religion and philosophy are built. The quest for answers to these questions is universal, but it is also personal, and as such, is always unique.

I had long ago sloughed off the anthropomorphic image of the Old Testament Yahweh. I had been taught the Father concept of Jesus. From physics I had tried to understand what is meant by creative energy, light, and harmony, and in time I came to envision a source of cosmic power I could plug into. Fortunately, I did not stop there.

The last decade has brought a tremendous upsurge in the search for truth—for God. After much reading and meditation, I arrived at my own concept (always subject to a revision, of course, and always inadequately expressed in words). It closely parallels the ecologist's idea that God is *the* Creative Energy, expressing Itself in everything on this planet—as plants, as trees, as rocks, as animals, as humans; yes, as every individual, even as me. This is not so much pantheism as recognition of the source of all creation, thus binding us all together as children of one creator, one father, and thus related. If this be true, and I believe it is, then it follows that for me to make contact with that power, I must not look "out there" but must turn within to that God-given spark of life implanted in me at birth, which I have come to call the Christ-within.

For a person of my generation this is a revolutionary shift, but one that illumines amd makes sense of Jesus' teachings. It gives importance to all life and provides for me a working philosophy.

To my grandchildren I would say: Read widely, think deeply. At different ages one needs different signposts. Maxims and quotations help keep one on course. Saints and sages have left us a rich heritage of distilled wisdom. Modern psychology is merely rephrasing Socrates' "Know thyself." A memorized line from a Psalm can act as a life jacket. When you come to a thought that "clicks," seize it and test it out. But until you discover your own, give mine a try:

> God rest you merry, gentlemen
> *Let nothing you dismay*,
> Remember Christ our Saviour
> Was born on Christmas Day.

God bless!

Signed: Grandmother

A Gift from the Mountains

I was raking leaves, my favorite chore, and wondering how the slender branches overhead could have supported the weight of all the leaves I was carrying in a burlap bag to the compost pile, when a shiny new car came whizzing up my steep driveway. A young couple got out and came toward me. I hadn't the faintest idea who they were but took off my work gloves and went to greet them.

"I'm Peter," said the young man. "Remember me? And this is my wife, Janet." I noted the pride of a newlywed in his introduction as Janet hastily added, "We stopped by to thank you in person for the lovely hand-woven table mats you sent us for a wedding present."

Then, of course, I remembered. Peter was the son of a good friend, a former city neighbor. She had brought him for a visit many years before—perhaps ten or twelve. He had grown to be a handsome straight-shouldered man, but I recalled the skinny, dark-haired boy of eleven, whose eyes always seemed to be asking questions. His wife was a trim blonde with a positive tilt to her chin. "Coming to the mountains for our honeymoon was Peter's idea," she said. "He talks about the mountains as if he owns them. I'm a seacoast person. I love the ocean."

"I love the ocean, too," I hastened to reply, sensing in her tone the beginnings of a private tug-of-

65

war between them, "but I also love the mountains. It isn't a case of either/or. And you are right about Peter owning a mountain. I gave him one years ago. Remember, Peter?"

Peter grinned. "What's more, you let me take it home with me, and after a while it started talking, just the way you said it would."

"I'm sure I don't know what you're talking about," said Janet, who would have changed the subject, but I said, "Go look at your mountain again, Peter, while Janet and I get acquainted."

I began by asking lots of questions, and Janet told me how she and Peter had met at the university— that successful matrimonial bureau—and after graduation they had waited till both had jobs and a tiny house before getting married, which was only three days before.

Peter did not stay away from his bride long and returned, saying, "That mountain doesn't look a thing like a camel. I wonder how I happened to think that."

"That's the price you pay for an A.B. degree. It put a quietus on your little-boy imagination. But I am happy you remembered it."

He was quick to say, "I not only remembered it, but I actually kept that picture you told me to make, and whenever I was alone, I used to talk things out. You were right. I almost always got the answers I wanted."

"Keep up the good work," I said, "and stop by to see me *and* your mountain whenever you can."

They made their adieus and I sent them off with my blessing. As I resumed raking, the whole scene, enacted twelve years earlier, was played back in my mind. Peter's mother had asked me to keep him while she made an emergency visit to Atlanta. I immediately launched him into making cookies, an undertaking that always provides an incentive. Peter stirred and dropped the batter by spoonfuls onto cookie sheets, but I sent him outside while I baked them in my temperamental oven. "Go on the side terrace and pick out the mountain you like best."

He was back in a jiffy. "I like the one that looks like a camel lying down."

"Then you can have it," I told him. "I'll give it to you. It's yours."

"But you can't give it to me 'cause you don't own it."

"Who says so? Nobody can take it away from where it is. It's mine to look at and talk to whenever I wish."

"Mountains can't talk."

"That's what *you* think."

"But they haven't got mouths to talk with."

"You're right, but there are other ways of communicating. How does your dog tell you he's glad you're home from school?"

"He jumps up on me and wags his tail. Mountains can't do that."

"Neither can trees or flowers or rocks, but they have their own way of talking. Mountains are a lot older and it takes them longer to answer your questions."

"Can I ask my mountain a question?"

I was glad he had already assumed ownership. "What do you want to ask it?"

"I want to know what I'm going to be when I grow up: a pilot like my daddy was, or a fireman, or maybe a president."

The first batch of cookies came out of the oven and he took a handful with him. He was back shortly for another sample. "That mountain didn't say a thing."

"I didn't much think it would," I consoled him. "Mountains take their time."

"But I'm going home tomorrow."

"Then I'll tell you what you can do. Go look real hard at your mountain. Then close your eyes. Can you remember *everything* about it? No. Then open your eyes and look again. Do this three or four times until you know *exactly* what your mountain looks like. You will have created your own mountain. Put a frame around it, pack it up, and take it home with you tomorrow."

Peter's eyes widened, and I could tell he was playing my game as he raced back to give it a try.

What I had been saying to Peter wasn't mere child's play. It was good psychology. Having a pictured place of beauty into which one can retreat in the midst of everyday life has been recommended from time immemorial. "He that dwelleth in the secret place of the most high, shall abide under the shadow of the Almighty." It has profound implications and is eminently useful.

I would say to all the visitors who come to the mountains, by all means take home gifts; patronize budding arts, buy ceramics, paintings, quilts, weaving, or cornshuck dolls; but better still, copy Peter. Carry away your own private replica of some special view. Stamp it indelibly so it can be a ready asylum at any time, anywhere. Let this be your own secret gift from the mountains.